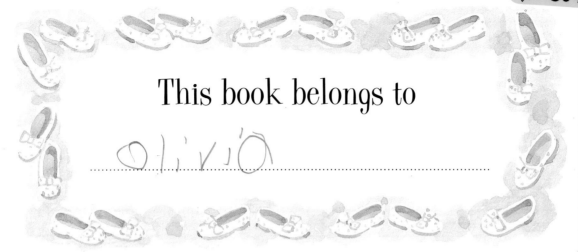

This book belongs to

Olivia

Sandy Creek
122 Fifth Avenue
New York, NY 10011

ISBN 978-1-4351-1162-2

10 9 8 7 6 5 4 3 Lot
Manufactured 8/18/2010
Manufactured in China

The Wizard of Oz

Written by L. Frank Baum
Retold by Gaby Goldsack
Illustrated by Shelagh McNicholas

Sandy Creek

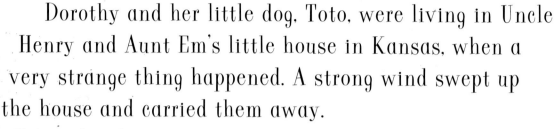

Dorothy and her little dog, Toto, were living in Uncle Henry and Aunt Em's little house in Kansas, when a very strange thing happened. A strong wind swept up the house and carried them away.

Hour after hour passed, and then the wind set the house down in a beautiful, magical land. As Dorothy opened the door and looked around, a group of strange little people appeared. One woman bowed before Dorothy.

"I am the Good Witch of the North," she said. "I would like to thank you for killing the Wicked Witch of the East, and setting us free."

"I have not killed anyone," gasped Dorothy.

"Well, your house did," replied the good witch. And she pointed to two red shoes sticking out from the corner of the house.

"Oh, dear! Oh, dear!" cried Dorothy.

"Don't worry, she was a very wicked witch," explained the good witch. "Now her magic shoes are yours. She was very proud of them but no one knows how they work. Here, put them on."

As Dorothy put on the shoes, she asked the good witch if she knew the way back to Kansas. The good witch and the little people looked at each other and shook their heads. None of them had even heard of Kansas.

"You will have to go to the Emerald City and ask Oz," said the good witch. "He is a great wizard. He will know how you can get back to Kansas."

"How do I get to the Emerald City?" asked Dorothy.

"Just follow the yellow brick road," said one of the little people.

Dorothy and Toto, quickly found the yellow brick road and began their journey. After they'd been walking for a long time they stopped beside a scarecrow for a rest. You can imagine Dorothy's surprise when the scarecrow winked and said, "Good day. Do you mind helping me down from this pole?"

After recovering from her surprise, Dorothy helped the scarecrow down. The scarecrow was very pleased. And when he heard that Dorothy was on her way to see the Wizard of Oz, he asked if he could come too.

"Perhaps he could give me some brains to replace the straw in my head," said the scarecrow.

So Dorothy, Toto and the scarecrow continued walking along the yellow brick road.

After a while, the road began to wind through some woods. Deep in some woods, Dorothy saw something glint among the trees. It was a man made of tin. He couldn't move because his joints were rusted solid.

"Help!" groaned the tinman. "Get that oil can and oil my joints."

Dorothy quickly did as he asked and soon the tinman could move once more.

"Where are you going?" asked the tinman, after he had thanked them at least a hundred times.

"To the Emerald City to see the Wizard of Oz," explained Dorothy. "He's going to send me back to Kansas."

"And he's going to give me a brain," added the scarecrow.

"Do you think the wizard could give me a heart?" asked the tinman.

"I expect so," said Dorothy.

"Then I'll come too," he decided.

Dorothy, Toto, the scarecrow, and the tinman were walking through the forest when they heard a terrible roar. Then a huge lion jumped out and knocked the scarecrow to the ground. Toto raced up barking and the terrible lion opened his jaws to bite him. Dorothy rushed forward and slapped the lion on the nose.

"You coward!" she cried. "You should be ashamed, a great beast like you trying to bite a tiny dog."

"I know I'm a coward," sobbed the lion. "I can't help it. Everyone expects me to be brave but I'm just a big scaredy cat. I just haven't got any courage."

"Perhaps Oz could give you courage," suggested the scarecrow. Then they explained how they were all on their way to the Emerald City to seek Oz's help. The lion quickly decided to join them and they set off once more.

The friends continued their journey until they came to a glowing green city. They had arrived at the Emerald City. Dorothy rang a bell and the gate swung open. A soldier stood before them.

"I am the guardian of the gate," said the man. "What do you want?"

"We've come to see the Wizard of Oz," explained Dorothy.

"I hope you have a good reason," said the little man. "Oz is a great but terrible wizard. He rules the Emerald City wisely and well. But if you are dishonest or just plain nosey, he could destroy you. Few have ever dared to ask to see his face. I will take you but you must take great care."

They all followed the soldier through the city to the Palace of the Great Oz.

The soldier went to tell the great Oz that he had visitors. When he returned he told Dorothy and her friends that Oz would see them one at a time.

Dorothy went into the throne room first. In the middle of the room an enormous head floated above an emerald throne.

"I am Oz, the great and terrible," roared the head. "What do you want?"

"I am Dorothy the small and meek. I want you to send me back to Kansas."

"I will, if you kill the Wicked Witch of the West, like you did the Wicked Witch of the East," said the head.

"But I killed the Wicked Witch of the East by accident," wailed Dorothy. "How can I kill a witch?"

"I don't know," replied the head. "But don't come back until you do."

Feeling very sad, Dorothy went back to tell her friends what the wizard wanted her to do.

The next day, the scarecrow went to see Oz. When he entered the throne room, he saw a beautiful lady sitting on the emerald throne. When he asked her for brains, she told him that he must help Dorothy kill the Wicked Witch of the West.

The tinman entered the throne room next. This time, the wizard appeared as a terrible beast, with five eyes and a huge woolly body. When the tinman asked for a heart, he was also told that he must help Dorothy kill the Wicked Witch of the West.

Next came the lion. He saw the wizard as a huge ball of fire. The ball of fire told the lion that if he wanted courage he must destroy the Wicked Witch of the West.

The lion rushed from the room to tell his friends what the wizard had said.

"We will have to do as he asks," decided Dorothy, "or we will never get what we want."

"Good luck," said the gatekeeper, pointing out the path to the witch's castle.

As they entered the strange country, they didn't realize that they were being watched. The Wicked Witch of the West had only one eye but it was as powerful as a telescope. When she saw the uninvited guests, she was furious. She put on a golden cap and said slowly, "Ziz-zy, zuz-zy, zik!" A crowd of winged monkeys immediately surrounded the witch.

"Destroy the tinman and the scarecrow," she commanded.
"And bring me the others."
The winged monkeys quickly found
Dorothy and her friends. Some seized
the tinman and the scarecrow and
dropped them into a deep ravine.
Others caught Dorothy, Toto,
and the lion and carried them
back to the witch's castle.

The witch was very frightened when she saw that Dorothy was wearing the Wicked Witch of the East's red shoes. She knew they were very powerful. But then she realized that Dorothy didn't know how to use their power and decided to steal them.

The witch said some magic words to make Dorothy fall over. As Dorothy stumbled, one of her red shoes flew off and the witch snatched it up. Dorothy was so angry that she threw a bucket of water over the witch. The witch shrieked with fear and began to melt away. Soon all that was left of her was a brown puddle.

When the witch's slaves saw that the Wicked Witch of the West was dead, they rescued the tinman and the scarecrow. Then Dorothy used the witch's golden cap to get the winged monkeys to take her and her friends back to the Emerald City.

When the friends rushed into Oz's throne room a great voice spoke to them.

"I am Oz, the great and terrible. What do you want?"

"We have destroyed the Wicked Witch of the West," said Dorothy. "Now we want what you promised us."

"Err…come back tomorrow," said the voice.

Hearing this, the lion roared. Toto jumped in alarm and knocked over a screen to reveal a little man.

"Who are you?" cried the tinman.

"I am Oz, the great and terrible," squeaked the little man. "Or rather I've been pretending to be. Really, I'm just a man who accidentally flew to Oz in a hot air balloon."

"So you won't be able to give us the things you promised," cried Dorothy.

"Don't worry," said the little old man. "I can still help you." And he gave the scarecrow a special stuffing for brains. He gave the tinman a red silk heart. And he gave the lion a drink to give him courage.

"How will I get to Kansas?" asked Dorothy.

"We'll fly there in my hot air balloon," said the little man.

The following day, Dorothy, Toto and the wizard climbed into a hot air balloon. The wizard waved to his people. "I'm going on vacation," he told them. "While I am gone, the scarecrow will rule over you."

As the balloon started to rise, Toto jumped out of the basket and Dorothy jumped out after him. There was no stopping the balloon. It flew away, leaving Dorothy and Toto behind. Dorothy was very sad.

"I'll never see Uncle Henry and Aunt Em again," she sobbed.

Then suddenly, a good witch appeared.

"I am the Good Witch of the South," she smiled. "How can I help you?"

"Help me get back to Kansas," said Dorothy.

"Your red shoes will carry you there," said the witch. "Just knock the heels together three times and ask them to take you wherever you wish."

Dorothy thanked the good witch and kissed each of her friends goodbye. Then she picked up Toto and tapped her shoes together three times, saying, "Take me home to Aunt Em!"

Instantly, she was whirled through the air and the next thing she knew she was back home in Kansas. Dorothy's adventure was over at last.

Aunt Em dropped her watering can and rushed over.

"Aunt Em!" cried Dorothy, "I'm so glad to be home."